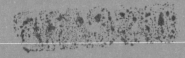

GOOD NIGHT, BUNNY

by Lauren Thompson • pictures by Stephanie Yue

Orchard Books • New York • An Imprint of Scholastic Inc.

Good night, sun and bright red sky.

Good night, swallows swooping by.

Good night, bluebells
and nodding pansies.

Good night, dainty dozy daisies.

Good night, spider

and flickering fireflies.

Good night, delicate dragonflies.

Good night, turtledove coo-cooing low.

Good night, ducklings in a row.

Good night, log and splashy creek.

Good night, mousies all a-squeak.

Good night, cattails
and moonlight glow.

Good night, minnows swimming slow.

Good night, breezes and clouds that fly.

Good night, twinkling stars up high.

Good night, crickets
cricking near.

Good night, Mama
and Papa dear.

Good night, brothers big and little.

Good night, sister snug in the middle.

Good night, ears

and whiskery nose.

Good night, wiggly tickly toes.

Good night, you, and good night, me.

Good night kisses one, two, three.

One last hug,
all tucked in tight.

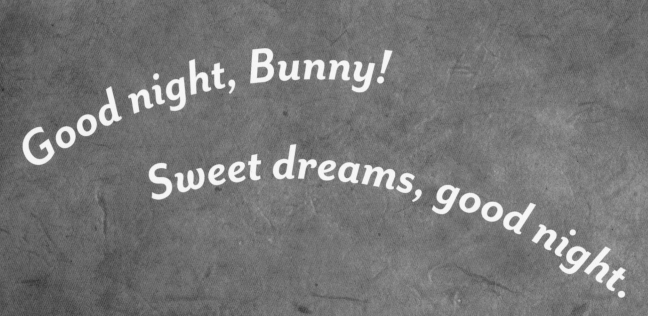

Good night, Bunny!

Sweet dreams, good night.

All rights reserved. Published by Orchard Books, an imprint of Scholastic Inc., *Publishers since 1920.* ORCHARD BOOKS and design are
registered trademarks of Watts Publishing Group, Ltd., used under license. SCHOLASTIC and associated logos are trademarks and/or
registered trademarks of Scholastic Inc.

Library of Congress Cataloging-in-Publication Data available
ISBN 978-0-545-60335-5

10 9 8 7 6 5 4 3 2 1   18 19 20 21 22
Printed in China 38   First edition, February 2018

The text type was set in Mr Eaves Sans Bold. The display type was set in Beach Tar Black.
Book design by Charles Kreloff and David Saylor